Prairie Willow

Story by Maxine Trottier
Paintings by Laura Fernandez and Rick Jacobson

TORONTO • NEW YORK

Published in Canada in 1998 by
Stoddart Kids,
a division of Stoddart Publishing Co. Limited
34 Lesmill Road
Toronto, Canada M3B 2T6
Tel (416) 445-3333 Fax (416) 445-5967
E-mail Customer.Service@ccmailgw.genpub.com

Distributed in Canada by
General Distribution Services
30 Lesmill Road
Toronto, Canada M3B 2T6
Tel (416) 445-3333 Fax (416) 445-5967
E-mail Customer.Service@ccmailgw.genpub.com

Published in the United States in 1998 by
Stoddart Kids
a division of Stoddart Publishing Co. Limited
180 Varick Street, 9th Floor
New York, New York 14207
Toll free 1-800-805-1083
E-mail gdsinc@genpub.com

Distributed in the United States by
General Distribution Services
85 River Rock Drive, Suite 202
Buffalo, New York 14207
Toll free 1-800-805-1083
E-mail gdsinc@genpub.com

Published in paperback in 1999 by Stoddart Kids

Canadian Cataloguing in Publication Data

Trottier, Maxine
Prairie willow

ISBN 0-7737-3067-2 (bound) ISBN 0-7737-6100-4 (pbk.)

I. Fernandez, Laura. II. Jacobson, Rick.
III. Title.

PS8589.R685P72 2000 jC813'.54 C97-931839-4
PZ7.T76Pr 2000

The Canada Council for the arts since 1957 | Le Conseil des Arts du Canada depuis 1957

We acknowledge for their financial support of our publishing program the Canada Council, the Ontario Arts Council, and the Government of Canada through the Book Publishing Industry Development Program (BPIDP).

Printed and bound in Hong Kong by
Book Art Inc., Toronto

For Den and Lynda
— Maxine

To immigrants, then and now,
who came understanding the promise
and carrying the hope —
our parents and grandparents among them.
— Laura and Rick

When Emily first saw the prairie she thought of a green-gold ocean. There they sat in the wagon, Emily, Papa, and Mama with Jack on her knee.

Their wagon was a boat with the waves of grass flowing around it. "This is it," said Papa, checking his map. "This is our homestead." And so it began.

They built a house from the earth. Like moles, Mama and Papa dug the sod and piled it up. Emily fed the chickens and played with Jack. At night they slept in the wagon. It rocked gently in the wind like a ship in the dark. Emily held her doll closely and dreamed of trees.

When the sod house was finished, Papa began to plough. There was wheat to sow and a kitchen garden to plant.

Emily followed Papa and the horses as long lines of furrows etched into the prairie. She helped Mama tuck beans and corn into the black earth.

That summer the land came to life around Emily. Sometimes she climbed to the roof of the sod house and looked over the plains. The house was a small island in the whispering grass. All day she could hear the sound of the wind on the prairie. At night in her dreams, the rustle of willows and birches called to her.

That fall the wheat was scythed and Papa took it away in the wagon for threshing. The money it earned would buy wood for a barn in spring.

“But there is a little extra,” he said to Emily. “What do you think we need?” They got out the old catalog. Emily turned the pages; then she stopped.

“This is what we need,” she said.

Mama helped her print the order. The next day Papa took it to town. Small flakes of snow were falling when he returned home that evening.

"Winter is coming," said Mama. And so it did. The prairie turned into a sea of white. Wind howled around the sod house but inside they were safe and warm. All that winter Emily watched and waited. Finally one day when the world dripped and melted, a neighbor stopped by.

"This came for you some weeks ago," he said. Then he clucked to his horse and rode away. Emily unwrapped the package and smiled. It was her tree.

Jacobson Fernandez

“It’s a weeping willow,” said Mama, reading the little tag. “When the ground is warm enough we will plant it.” And they did. Papa dug the hole and Mama lowered in the little tree. Emily and Jack patted soil around its roots.

Slowly, slowly the tree grew. By the time Emily was old enough to walk to the schoolhouse, it was as high as her head. When Jack was old enough to go with her, Emily had to look up to see the leaves at its top. Then one summer it was big enough for all of them to sit under. That fall, its leaves scattered and danced over the prairie. Its bare branches stood out against the gray sky.

When Jack went away to be a soldier, Emily and Mama stood under the tree and watched Papa drive him to the train station. And when the telegram came telling them how brave Jack had been to fight and die for his country, Emily sat alone behind the willow's green veil and cried.

All her life, Emily had the prairie willow. In a world that constantly changed it was the one thing that stayed the same. Mama and Papa grew too old to farm and left the land to her. Emily married and had children. They married and did the same. Emily's grandchildren would come to visit.

"One time there was a twister," she sometimes told them. "Your Great Uncle Jack and I saw it pass by." Then she would show them the place where the branch had broken. The tree had held onto the prairie, its roots sunk deep in the black dirt.

One night when she was very old, Emily had a dream. In the dream she was small again. She stood on the roof of the old sod house and looked out across the prairie. It seemed as though she was high in the crow's nest of a ship looking for a lost sailor on the grassy sea. The wind blew her braids straight out behind her. Then she saw him. Far away on the prairie stood Jack. Emily could see her brother's long ago smile in the sunlight. She climbed off the sod house and ran to meet him. And so it ended.

Some nights when the wind blows hard, the willow bends and sways. Leaves skitter into the darkness and its branches creak, but the tree is part of the earth. That is the way of things on the prairie. Held firmly to the land by its roots and a dream, the willow stands there still.